A

IS FOR AMOUR

A is for Amour, edited by Alison Tyler, is available from www.cleispress.com.

B

IS FOR BONDAGE

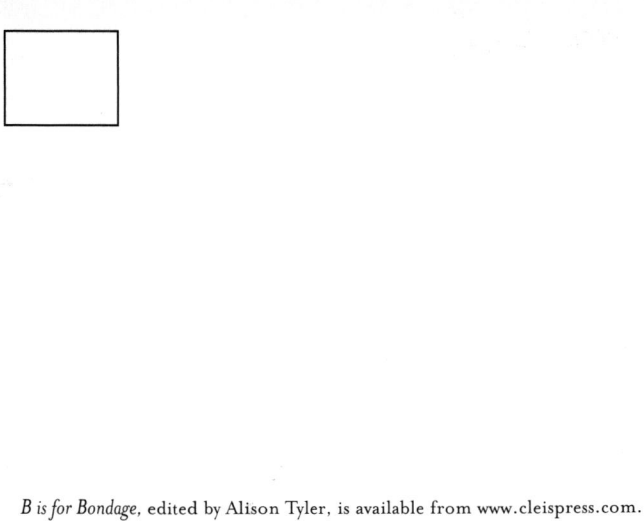

B is for Bondage, edited by Alison Tyler, is available from www.cleispress.com.

IS FOR CO-EDS

C is for Coeds, edited by Alison Tyler, is available from www.cleispress.com.

IS FOR DRESS-UP

D is for Dress-Up, edited by Alison Tyler, is available from www.cleispress.com.

IS FOR EXOTIC

E is for Exotic, edited by Alison Tyler, is available from www.cleispress.com.

IS FOR FETISH

F is for Fetish, edited by Alison Tyler, is available from www.cleispress.com.

G IS FOR GAMES

H IS FOR HARDCORE

H is for Hardcore, edited by Alison Tyler, is available from www.cleispress.com.

IS FOR INDECENT

I is for Indecent, edited by Alison Tyler, is available from www.cleispress.com.

IS FOR Jealousy

J is for Jealousy, edited by Alison Tyler, is available from www.cleispress.com.

IS FOR KINKY

L IS FOR LEATHER

L is for Leather, edited by Alison Tyler, is available from www.cleispress.com.

IS FOR master

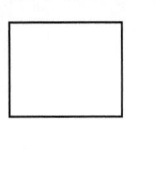

M is for Master, edited by Alison Tyler, is available from www.cleispress.com.

N IS FOR NAUGHTY

IS FOR ORGASM

O is for Orgasm, edited by Alison Tyler, is available from www.cleispress.com.

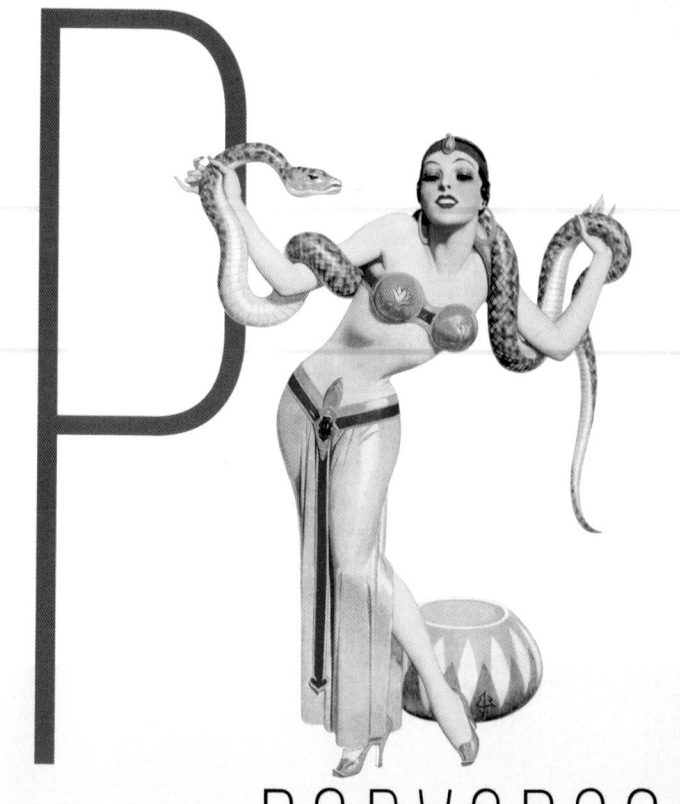

P

IS FOR PERVERSE

P is for Perverse, edited by Alison Tyler, is available from www.cleispress.com.

IS FOR QUICKIE

Q is for Quickie, edited by Alison Tyler, is available from www.cleispress.com.

R

IS FOR Raunchy

R is for Raunchy, edited by Alison Tyler, is available from www.cleispress.com.

T

IS FOR TRASHY

T is for Trashy, edited by Alison Tyler, is available from www.cleispress.com.

IS FOR UNDERWEAR

U is for Underwear, edited by Alison Tyler, is available from www.cleispress.com.

IS FOR VOYEUR

V is for Voyeur, edited by Alison Tyler, is available from www.cleispress.com.

Copyright © 2008 Scott Idleman.

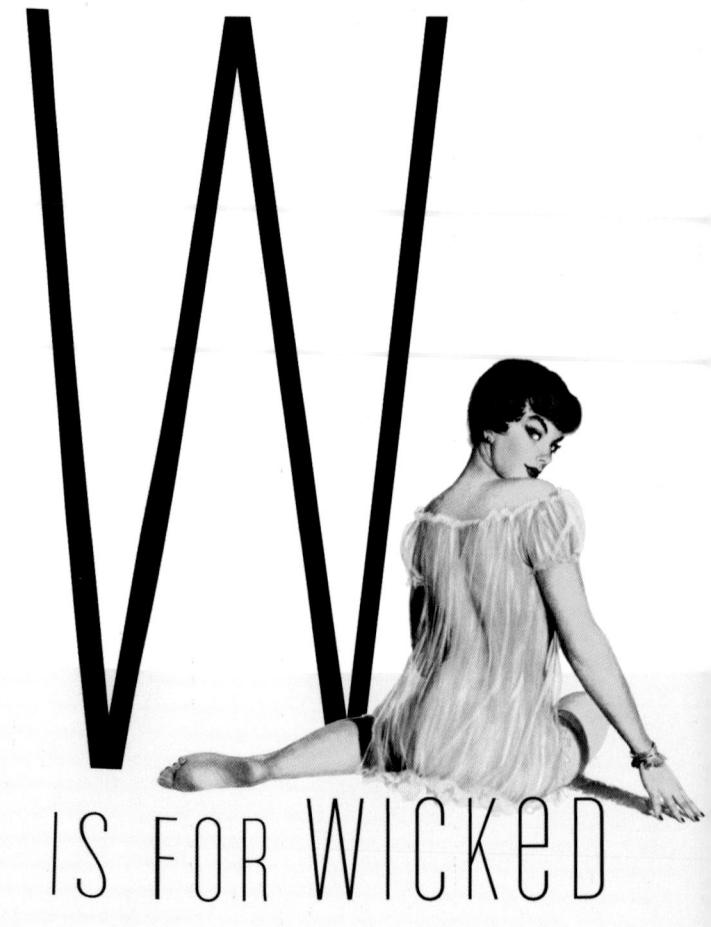

W IS FOR WICKED

W is for Wicked, edited by Alison Tyler, is available from www.cleispress.com.

IS FOR X-RATED

X is for X-Rated, edited by Alison Tyler, is available from www.cleispress.com.